# Miss Otter Goes To The Movies

## Gary Richmond

Dallas • London • Sydney • Singapore

VIEW FROM THE ZOO STORIES are based on the real-life adventures of Gary Richmond, a veteran of the Los Angeles Zoo, minister, counselor, and camp nature speaker. Gary has three children and lives in Chino Hills, California, with his wife, Carol.

Printed in the United States of America

012349LB98765432

**Library of Congress Cataloging-in-Publication Data**

Richmond, Gary, 1944-
    Miss Otter goes to the movies / by Gary Richmond ;
    illustrated by Bruce Day.
    p. cm. (A View from the zoo series)
    Summary: A Christian zookeeper relates an anecdote
about an otter he tried to tame and draws a parallel
with the teaching that only God can tame the tongue.
    ISBN 0-8499-0743-8 : $7.99
    1. Oral communication — Religious aspects —
Christianity. 2. Clean speech — Juvenile literature.
[1. Christian life. 2. Otters. 3. Zoos.] I. Day, Bruce, ill.
II. Title. III. Series: Richmond, Gary, 1944- View from
the zoo series.
BV4597.53.C64R53 1990
242'.62 — dc20                                        90-12344
                                                              CIP
                                                              AC

*This book is dedicated to my daughter Marci, who like Miss Otter, knows there's no biz like show biz.*

Hi, I'm Gary Richmond, and I'm a zoo keeper. As a zoo keeper I've learned a lot about God's wonderful animals. At the same time, I've also learned a lot about God.

I'd like to tell you about one animal that became a special friend to me — an otter named Girl.

It all started on my very first day as a zoo keeper. I began as the keeper of the animals in the aquatics (that means water) area of the zoo. And I had a lot to learn about wild animals.

On that first day Al, my boss and the senior zoo keeper, told me this: "Gary, a good zoo keeper knows that it's important to let wild animals stay wild. Don't try to tame them or make them into pets. If you do, both you and the animals will be unhappy. They will no longer be what God wants them to be."

Most of the water animals didn't make good pets anyway. So it was easy to follow the "no pet" rule most of the time. Sometimes I did wish I could make friends with the otters. They were so active, curious and playful. One lady otter would stand at the gate and watch me prepare their food or clean their area. She looked as if she would like to make friends, too. But I remembered Al's warning; so, I kept my distance.

One day Fred, Al's boss, came to see me. He said, "Gary, how would you like to try to tame that friendly lady otter of yours? A Hollywood movie director wants to use an otter for a movie premier two months from now. You don't have to teach her to do tricks. Just get her so she won't bite anyone."

It sounded like fun, and I agreed to try.

I began by going into the otters' area and sitting down quietly. I threw pieces of their favorite food near their pool. The food is a small sardine-like fish called smelt. Otters are curious animals; so, they all swam over to see what I had thrown to them. They noisily ate the fish and waited for more.

The friendly lady otter didn't eat her smelt right away. She swam around with it in her mouth. It was almost like a game to her. I softly said hello and asked if she was still hungry. She stared at me, wanting more fish. I threw her another piece, which she ate quickly.

Then I threw a piece of smelt half way between the lady otter and me. She took one careful step closer to the smelt and stopped. She wanted the fish. But she was afraid to come close enough to me to get it. So, she went back to the pool, looking hungrily at the smelt over her shoulder.

The next day I sat closer to the pool. I hoped she would feel safer in the water and come closer to get her smelt treats. It worked! Soon she was swimming just five feet from me to get her goodies. After two weeks she would come within one foot of my hand. We were making progress!

One afternoon, the lady otter surprised me by jumping out of the pool near me. She stood there with happy eyes waiting for her favorite treat.

So, I held out a whole smelt in my hand toward her.
She was a little scared, and so was I. I knew she might snap
at the fish and bite my hand. I held the smelt just two inches
from her face. She leaned over, opened her mouth and shut
it gently to take the treat.

Then she took hold of the smelt with her front paws
and ate it like an ice cream cone. It was a magical moment!

The next step to tame her was harder. I had to get her to sit on my lap. I started by laying smelt on the other side of my stretched-out legs from her. At first she walked around my legs to get it. Then she began climbing across them to the other side.

Finally, I held the smelt in front of my face. She jumped onto my lap. The otter put her front paws on my chest and took the fish in her mouth. Then she sat right on my lap and ate it.

Now that we were friends, I thought the lady otter should have a name. But I couldn't think of a really good name. I decided to just call her "Girl" until I could think of something better. After a week Girl seemed to fit her; so, Girl became her name.

The next day I worked with Girl again. This time, after eating her smelt she stayed on my lap to clean herself. She licked her paws, combed and oiled her hair. Then she curled up for a nap on my lap. I couldn't believe it! She finally trusted me.

When I saw Girl again, I tried to pet her. She yawned lazily and lay down in the sunshine to enjoy it. Then, for the first time, she played with me. She pretended to bite my hand gently and growled playfully. It was clearly a game, which we both enjoyed.

Finally, one day she let me pick her up and hold her. She snuggled against my shoulder, and I petted her gently. It was a wonderful day for both of us.

Time was going by quickly. It was getting closer and closer to the movie premier. I began to wonder if Girl would be tame enough in time. We still had a lot to do before she would be ready. So, we began all sorts of experiments with Girl. We took her riding in the car. We let other people pet her and trained her to wear a leash.

She didn't seem to care what kind of clothes or perfume we wore. She liked ladies, children and the other zoo keepers. It was only five days before the premier, and Girl seemed ready for her performance. So far she had passed her tests with flying colors. I was sure she would steal the show in Hollywood.

The day of the premier came; and I was nervous. Girl was perky and lovable as usual. The television crew was coming to film Girl at the zoo that morning. Girl was used to having her picture taken by zoo visitors. So, I thought this would be good practice for her evening show.

Suddenly I saw Fred running toward me. He was out of breath and looked worried.

"What's up, Fred?" I asked.

"One of the television directors wants to have a chimpanzee with Girl in today's news story," he said. "I tried to talk them out of it. But I couldn't get them to change their minds. They will be here any minute."

I had a sick feeling in my stomach. We had not tested Girl with other animals. I knew in my heart that she was not ready for such a surprise.

Soon the television crew began to arrive. I stood by holding Girl. I wanted to be holding her when the chimp arrived. When he came into the area, Girl knew it right away. She jumped out of my arms and ran to her pool. She watched the hairy little guy carefully to see if he would try to hurt her. Then she crawled out of the pool. She slowly walked between the visitors to get a closer look at him.

The chimp was holding hands with the zoo keeper. He looked just like a hairy baby out for a walk with his father. When the chimp saw Girl, he screamed and slapped at Girl with its hand. He was as scared of Girl as she was of him.

That was all Girl needed to know! Something dangerous had come into her world. There was no love in her eyes now. When I tried to pick her up, she growled at me. So, I just let her run around on the ground and watch the chimp.

Girl didn't act like a tame otter that day. The movie director was very unhappy with her. All I could do was say I was sorry and explain that Girl had never been around a chimpanzee before. Sixty days of hope and hard work seemed ruined. Then I remembered that this was only a practice run. We still had the premier and movie stars to entertain that evening. Maybe things would turn out all right after all.

The chimp and people finally left the otters' area. I stayed behind to try to calm Girl. But she was still upset. By five o'clock she still wouldn't let me pick her up. We had to leave for Hollywood in fifteen minutes. At last, I held her while Al tried to put her leash on. She gave me a dirty look and bit Al's arm.

We couldn't trust Girl not to bite someone else that night. So we had to take her to the premier in a small cage. She was not happy in the cage and paced back and forth the whole evening. Girl didn't look at all like a tame otter.

We got back to the zoo late that night. Girl ran out of the cage to join her sleeping friends. She looked at me kindly for several seconds, but she was very tired. I wondered what an otter thinks when she has been treated gently for so many days and then her world turns upside down.

Al had been right at the beginning, and now I remembered his wise words: "Don't try to turn wild animals into pets."

I whispered, "Goodnight, Girl. Sorry."

Then I went home a sadder but wiser zoo keeper. In the weeks that followed, I gently helped Girl become a wild animal again. I was not surprised that she became happier, too. She was once again what God wanted her to be.

Taming Girl seemed like a difficult thing to do at the time. Since then I have played with tame wolves, coyotes, foxes, snow leopards and pythons. I have seen tame lions, jaguars, bears and apes. So, I was surprised one day to read this in my Bible:

> People can tame every kind of wild animal, bird, reptile, and fish...But no one can tame the tongue" (James 3:7, ICB).

God said that no one has enough power to control his own tongue. It's like having a wild animal loose right in your mouth!

That's the bad news; but here's the good news: God can help you tame your tongue, if you will ask him. God can help you control what you say so that you don't hurt people.

Maybe you have a problem telling lies. If so, God will help you tell the truth. Maybe you can't stop saying mean things about others. God will help you find nice things to say about them. If you use bad language, God will help you stop. If you complain too much, God will help you feel happier.

God is the greatest tamer who's ever lived. He can tame the meanest critter of all — the tongue! You'll be happier, and so will God when you are the person he wants you to be. Won't you let him help you tame your tongue?